Brian Was Adopted

The story by DORIS SANFORD
Illustrations by GRACI EVANS

MULTNOMAH

10209 SE Division Street Portland, Oregon 97266

*To Gail Grimston,
mother of the year*

My parents wanted to adopt a baby. One day they got a phone call from the agency and someone asked if they would like a little Korean boy. They said they would love one, so that's how they got me.

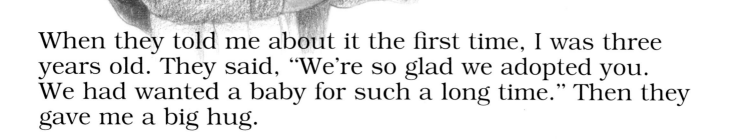

When they told me about it the first time, I was three years old. They said, "We're so glad we adopted you. We had wanted a baby for such a long time." Then they gave me a big hug.

Dear God,
It's kind of hard to understand that I have another set of parents somewhere, but I know I belong with my adoptive parents. Children grow better in families, all kinds of families.
Love,
Brian

Someone always asks me, "Are you really brothers?" I say, "Yes, we really are." Looking like Mom and Dad is not a requirement for their love. My brother isn't more special than me though. Mom and Dad love us both the same.

Even though I'm adopted, and on top of that a completely different race from my parents and brother, it just never occurs to me that they aren't my real family.

Dear God,
Sometimes people ask my parents weird questions like, "Do you also have children of your own?" or "Why couldn't you get a white child?" They don't know that being adopted means being a "real" child forever. My grandpa says I was a gift from Korea. Thank you for the gift of love.

Your friend,
Brian

I have lots of questions too, such as, Why didn't my first mother keep me? Mom said she wanted to, but she couldn't take care of me because she was too young and poor. She wanted me to have the right care, so she took me to the adoption agency.

When I asked what my first mother was like, my dad
said, "She must have had some wonderful qualities to
have had you." They don't know exactly what she
looked like.

My mom said that when they were standing at the airport arrival gate and I was placed in her arms for the first time, well, she still can't talk about it without crying.

Dear God,
I think about being adopted far more than my parents know. Sometimes I wish I could remember my birth parents, but all I know is what I've been told. I know my parents didn't just end up with me. I'm the son they always wanted. It's like I was lost and they found me. It's the same in Your family, huh?

Love,
Brian

My dad said he loves the ways that Michael and I are different. He said we both have messy rooms though. He doesn't tell people I'm adopted, because he forgets. But I can tell anyone I like.

Once when Dad punished me I said, "You're not my *real* Dad, so you can't tell me what to do." He said, "I love you, you're my son. Now go to your room!" And I never mentioned it again.

My mom saved the Korean clothes I wore when I came on the plane. I sure was little! One day I took the clothes and a copy of my birth certificate to school to Show and Tell.

My mom feels a close bond to my birth mother. Mom said, "It's sad that she won't be able to hear you sing or giggle."

Once, I asked my mom, "Why didn't you make your own baby?" She said, "We hadn't been able to have a baby before we adopted you. After you came, I became pregnant with Michael."

Before I was born, a neighbor said my parents were going to have a baby the "easy" way. But that's not true! They went to a lot of trouble to get me.

Dear God,
I know my parents had
to be special people
because the adoption
agency checked to be
sure they were good
enough for me. Thank
you for my family, God.
Love,
Brian

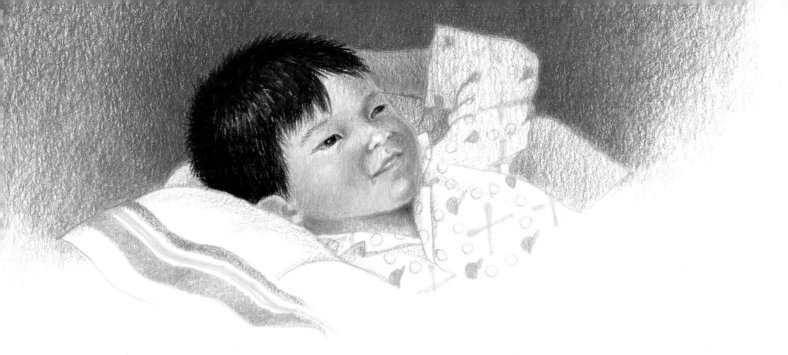

Sometimes at night I lay awake thinking about so many questions:

Do I have any brothers and sisters I don't know about?
Do my birth parents think about me on my birthday?

And, I'd like to know what kind of grades they got in school.

When I was little I always asked my mom, "Did I do something bad?" And she would show me a letter from the Korean agency that says, "He is a very good baby. We all love him." That always made me feel better. There was nothing about the kind of baby I was that made them give me up.

The day after my first birthday we went to court with
a lawyer to make everything legal. That means nobody
can take me away from my mom and dad.

I told my mom, "I wish I grew inside you." She said, "I wish so too, but that isn't what makes me your mom and you my child. I am your mom because:

1. We made a forever and ever promise to care for you.
2. Love is something you decide; it doesn't come automatically by being born. And . . .
3. We signed a paper that makes you legally ours.

Your dad and I *grew you in our hearts!*"

I was legally adopted December 3rd. My dad writes me a love letter every year on my adoption date and says a lot of mushy things about how much he loves me.

Someday I'd like to go to Korea. I want to say thank you to my birth mother and tell her I'm OK.

Sometimes I pretend my birth mother is a famous
singer. Actually, I don't know if she can sing at all. Once
we went to a Korean restaurant. I don't like Kimch'i.

I'm glad we live in a neighborhood with children of many races. My dad wants me to understand my heritage so he brings me books about Korea.

"We have decided to save the details of Brian's background for his ears only so that when he is old enough to understand, he can be in charge of how much he wants the world to know. We tell him over and over about the adoption. Telling him isn't a one-time event."